# MY GOD HIS NAMES

## A POETIC DESCRIPTION

RYAN "JENKS" JENKINS

JenRyan Co.
Inspiration • Motivation • Empowerment

## TABLE OF CONTENTS

## MY GOD, HIS NAMES INTRO

In my life, God has had many different names. Based on the challenge or victory I was facing, His name continued to change. He has showed up when I was lacking hope and struggled. God has been a supporter and the one I can call on. In the same way, there have been moments in my life where praise has overflowed from my lips. I know that God was the reason for the shower of blessings. I recognize it was not by my own actions.

I wanted to create a poetic way to express the many names in which God has showed up in my life, either as a rescuer from my obstacles or a giver of abundance. I will admit, in this book I have used God and Jesus interchangeably in some cases. It was hard to separate the two since both play a leading role in my faith and one can't be praised without the other. God is the giver of life and in all things. However, I would not be seen as righteous in God's eyes if it wasn't for Jesus' sacrifice which was the plan of God. Like I said, both need to be praised!

I hope you enjoy the poetry and quotes in this book. I want them to inspire, encourage, and strengthen you in your faith walk. I pray you see these names and recognize how God has impacted your life. I also hope that this book inspires the writers reading this to share their faith in a new way and more frequently. Writing these expressions has further inspired me in my craft and I hope it does the same for you. Please enjoy *My God, His Names*.

**"The name of Jesus is**

# LIGHT

**in the dark."**

## WATER WALKER

Nothing to separate You from me,
You would leave the shore and walk on the sea.
No matter where I am, You will come,
Now I know You are the One.

"My Water Walker"

Your love flows greater than any river,
Every time You come, You arrive to deliver.
Tears flow when I think about how much You care,
I'm broken Lord, but You are always ready to repair.

"My Water Walker"

Where my strength ends, Yours begins,
You chose me and forgave all of my past and future sins.
My experiences reveal You aren't just a talker,
You are the God of action, My Water Walker.

## SIGHT RELEASER

Darkness surrounds my view,
Lost in what I think is true.
Living for the moment, there is no tomorrow,
I see what's in front of me and no further.

Then a voice intrudes my space,
Peace is felt and a change of pace.
Comfort becomes my home,
I realize I am no longer alone.

All of sudden, the fog begins to descend,
Light becomes more recognizable from within.
Confusion now comes into focus,
Now I know the Sight Releaser is in my presence.

"Your

# FAITH

will take you places
beyond your dreams."

## SAVIOR

My God forgive me for what I have done,
I now know you are the only one.
Forgive me for all of my sins,
What I have said and thought within.

I confess with my mouth that Jesus is Lord of my life,
He died so my sins can be wiped from Your sight.
I believe in my heart through the tears I shed,
That You raised Jesus from the dead.

He now sits on the throne by Your side,
His blood was shed so my old ways could die.
I believe and proclaim that I am now saved,
Jesus is my Savior and He will direct my way.

Amen.

## TEACHER

Lesson after lesson do You teach,
Your wisdom flows from head to feet,
No one wiser than You can speak,
Wisdom is even in the air I breath.

You share without discrimination,
You teach me in every situation,
You even keep my feelings in consideration,
And Your love provides me confirmation.

What next will You give,
Another lesson on how to live,
What better ways will You reveal,
What remedies will You release to heal.

Your words touch my soul deeper and deeper,
Some will call You a true stress reliever,
The nuggets of knowledge You give are keepers,
That's why You will always be my teacher.

**"GOD**

**loves you."**

## HOPE GIVER

The world always needs hope,
We are joyous and troubled folk.
This journey has thrown challenges on the path,
Moments that remove the smiles and laughs.

"But You are a Hope Giver"

We try our best, yet sometimes fail,
But we live another day to share our tale.
The struggle becomes real to many of us,
Lack of true friends, not knowing who to trust.

"But You are a Hope Giver"

However, You have come to support our needs,
You plant hope as fertile seeds.
You tell us what is possible,
You bring a miracle to the impossible.

"But You are a Hope Giver"

You shine light in our dark,
You bring healing to our hurting parts.
You release forgiveness when we differ,
You are our God, the Hope Giver.

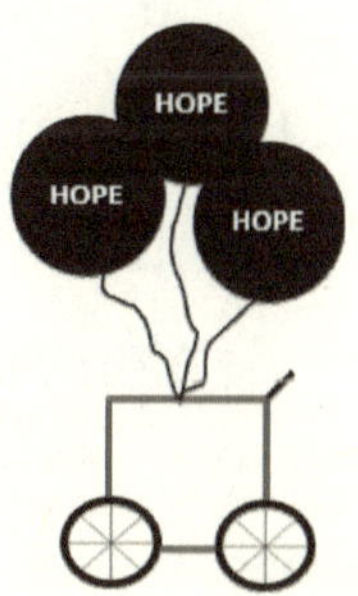

## ELEVATOR

From one level, You take me to the next,
I'm moving so fast, it leaves me perplexed.
I know I'm undeserving, but I continue to move,
With Your grace, I cannot lose.

It's like I'm dreaming with my eyes open,
And the blessings keep coming beyond what I have spoken.
More than I can imagine is what's ahead,
You persistently keep my dreams well fed.

Another level do I rise,
The Son is the reason I'm so high.
I know He has a plan for my future,
My Jesus, My King, My Elevator!

**"There is still a**

# PLAN

**for your life."**

## BEST FRIEND

You were there through my confusion,
You were there when wisdom wasn't what I was using.
You were there to forgive me when I did wrong,
You were there to introduce me to the Book of Psalms.

You were there when I would fall,
You were there to encourage and give me a call.
You were there when I doubted myself,
You were there when I felt no one was left.

You were there when I was treated unfair,
You were there like the morning air.
You were there when I needed the courage to not bend,
You were there Jesus, my closest and best friend.

## RIGHTEOUS

From on high God saw my sins,
He sent Jesus to save me from within.
Jesus took on flesh so in this world He could walk,
He would experience the sins and temptations of my walk.

From Mary's labor, Jesus was born,
Not in a palace, but a manger and the rumors began to form.
Some would say Jesus was supposed to be the Savior,
This revelation shifted some people's thoughts and behavior.

As Jesus grew, He was tested and He healed,
But that didn't stop His love and the miracles He would fulfill.
He was chased, denied and crossed,
However that didn't stop Him from dying on the cross.

Jesus died and rose for power over our sins,
He lived as an example that victory would be our win.
He sits beside God on our behalf,
He speaks for us when we struggle and have no laugh.

All we have to do is believe in Jesus and confess our sins,

Accept Jesus as our Savior and we are made right within.
So when we pray, we pray in Jesus' name,
God then sees our goodness when we mention Jesus' name.

Since we are right with Jesus, we are right with God,
Even though we may still struggle, God sees our heart.
We are on a journey to grow and do better,
And Jesus vouches for us in more than a letter.

Jesus' life and blood was proof of His belief in us,
Now God sees Jesus in all of us.
No more me alone, but me and Jesus,
He gave us a new name because He's righteous.

**"With Jesus, you are**

# NEVER

**alone."**

## LIGHTHOUSE

The waves of life begin to rage,
So dark, so confused I can't tell night from day.
It feels like I'm hit from all sides,
My fear I can no longer hide.

"I see a Lighthouse"

More rain falls and I'm going down,
My hope is fading with a face filled with frown.
Winds blowing from the east and west,
How much longer can I stand this test.

"I see a Lighthouse"

I see a glimpse from afar,
I headed starboard and turn really hard.
I'm not sure what it is, but I have no choice,
I need help or I'm going overboard.

"I see a Lighthouse"

Brighter and brighter the light becomes,
I better reach it before the big one comes.
As I get closer, it begins to get clearer out,
The waves start to dissipate as I reach the Lighthouse.

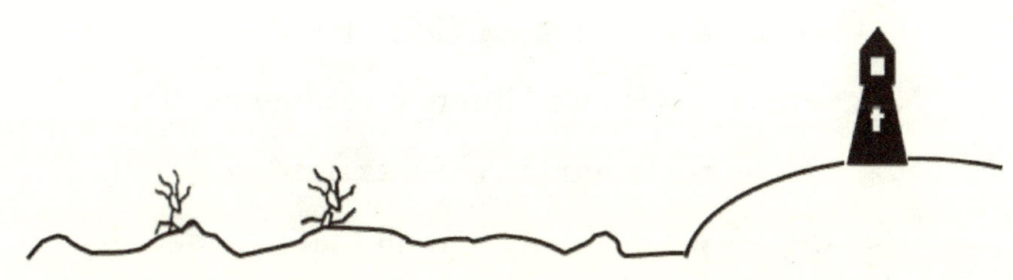

## MY REBUILDER

I may be broken, but I can be repaired,
God sees things that I don't think are there.
He takes my pieces and makes peace,
His love is all over me.

My Rebuilder

No task too big for God's hands,
No distance too far for Him to reach me on land.
He is never too far, close as needed,
No matter what I lose, He is all that I needed.

My Rebuilder

What's odd is perfect to Him,
What people judge about me is a gift from Him.
Each day I learn, grow and become better,
I will be made new because of My Rebuilder.

**"If you**

# **BELIEVE**

**you can change, then you can change!"**

## REPOSITIONER

This way shall I go to achieve my dream,
But what I see as great isn't what it seems.
I thought I wanted certain things for my life,
But You came in and showed me a new light.

"You are my Repositioner"

I thought my direction was so clear to the end,
Yet Your plan for me is bigger than I can comprehend.
You are a visionary like no other,
Your dream for me has no lid or cover.

"You are my Repositioner"

Now I am on a new path without a doubt,
I will follow you from the north to the south.
Your guidance comforts me and takes me further,
My future is blessed because You are my Repositioner.

## AMAZING

I don't want to get comfortable with the
amazing things You do,
I don't want to take for granted the blessings
coming from You.
I want to continue to be shocked and in awe,
Your plan comes on time without blemish or flaw.

"I don't want to get comfortable with Amazing"

You deliver when I least expect,
And it can come from a direction I never expect.
No plan of Yours is ever the same,
I guess that is defined in Your name.

"I don't want to get comfortable with Amazing"

There are no words to describe the feeling of You,
Knowing this moment is made possible because of You.
All of Your actions are worth praising,
I don't want to get comfortable, but
keep calling You Amazing.

**"No place in your life is too**

# DARK

**for God to go."**

## HERO

So many times we call people Heroes,
But that definition, do we really know.
We look at what they have and what they've done,
But let me tell you about a Hero beyond anyone.

A Hero that took on our sins,
A Hero that also fought battles within.
A Hero that has walked where we have been,
And in all of that, rose with Victory so we can win.

This Hero doesn't judge people by what
they physically possess,
He judges the heart where the greatest treasure is kept.
This Hero was shaped in Love,
His name is Jesus, a Hero from above.

## THE CREATOR

God made me inside and out,
I am His creation without a doubt.
I can't take credit for who I am,
God is much more than any man.

"I am wonderfully and marvelously made"

God had no flaws on me,
If I think so, it's because I can't see.
I can't see the perfection in His sight,
So I seek Him to get my eyes right.

"I am wonderfully and marvelously made"

I can't compare me to anyone else,
His design for me is like no one else.
He crafted and shaped me in His will,
There is no reason His purpose I can't fulfill.

"I am wonderfully and marvelously made"

I hope others feel the way I do,
No heads hung low, but being excited to be you.
My God, make sure I shine bright even in the shade,
God I praise You because I am wonderfully
and marvelously made.

WONDERFULLY AND

MARVELOUSLY MADE

**"Your path is by**
**DESIGN."**

**THE SHOEMAKER**

I want to walk in the shoes that you have planned for me,
Custom designed to fit my path and my feet.
I don't want to stroll anyone else's road,
I want my own destiny to grip and hold.

I am equipped for the journey I am assigned,
My shoes are made for the mountains I will have to climb.
They were shaped for the course I would take,
You made sure every curve, arch and the
material wouldn't go to waste.

You thought it out clearly like only You could do,
You saw my future and the things I would do.
Now I feel secure with Your design on my feet,
God, You are my shoemaker knowing what's best for me.

## WISE

God, You are all wise,
You see what's not in my eyes.
You know what's to come when I don't,
You know what I need to learn when I don't.

So many times I wonder what You see,
What is the better version of me.
But I Thank You for the wisdom You have shared,
You taught me things about life and money
that just come out of the air.

I have no doubt that You have a plan,
Even when I'm writing a book, I know it's Your hand.
But tell me when I go too far,
I don't want to do anything that's not my part.

Most important to me is Your will,
If it's doing books and teaching youth and adults, I will.
You know what's best for me,
Thank You for having wisdom I can't see.

**"What you**

# BELIEVE

**influences what**
**you see."**

## BELIEVER

You believe in me when I have doubt,
You encourage me when I am without.
You always see the best in me,
I am grateful You Believe in me.

You are my light when I go dark,
You are that energy that is my spark.
You are My God, the better part of me,
Thank You Lord for Believing in me.

## THE AUTHOR

The greatest book written is the Bible to me,
It tells you how to live and what to believe.
It brought together a unique group of writers,
The wisdom in its words will take you further.

It was all inspired or orchestrated by God,
He knows how to bring things out of the odd.
He is stated as the beginning and the end,
But it takes faith for you to comprehend.

Revelation after revelation, this book is packed,
Every time you read it, a new message is unwrapped.
There is no better book that is timeless and elevational,
Yes, it's the Holy Bible, the greatest book I know.

**"No one is**

# WISER

**than God."**

## GOD

You protect me through all that I face,
When I'm confused, You always make a way.
I may have doubt, but You are there,
You are my strength when I am scared.

"You are God"

You smile down on me with joy,
You raised me to a man from a boy.
You showed me how to have faith,
You showed me how I should pray.

"You are God"

There is no end to Your power,
You are there every minute and every hour.
Even when I think You left, You are here,
In those times, I heard You even nearer.

"You are God"

You are so worthy to be praised,
You are wiser than all of my days.
I don't know where I would be without You,
You are God and I'm a part You.

You are God..
You are God..
You are God.

## THE GUIDE

God, You are so wise,
When I'm lost, encouragement You provide.
You are there when I'm in need,
You provide guidance with speed.

You show me a way out,
You change my thoughts to a way out.
When I seem to be closed in,
You let me know there is another direction within.

Your wisdom answers any question that I may have,
Past or future, You have already done the math.
I Thank You for being my guide in this voyage,
Keep talking to my heart as we continue my voyage.

**"Opportunity is**

# WAITING

**on you."**

## THE WAITER

Bad decision after decision and You didn't worry,
My living was spicy like Jamaican curry.
My sins and me couldn't be separated,
But my God, You waited.

You waited for me to change,
You gave me Your wisdom and love, and now
I'm not the same.
You taught me about who I am,
You gave me purpose and guided me in Your plan.

My life will never be the same because of You,
You gave me value regardless of what I owned and what I do.
You empowered my faith and showed me favor,
You are my Savior Jesus Christ, The Waiter.

## ARTIST

If God was to paint my life, what would it be,
Would it be a traditional picture or abstract art you see.
Would there be lines large and small,
Splashes of color with drips and dots covering it all.

Would the strokes represent the events of my journey,
Would the hues define the roller coaster of
emotions that I breathe so easily.
I wonder how the masterpiece will play out,
I won't know until this voyage ends and I meet
the Artist to find out.

**"No child of God is**

# LEFT

**behind."**

**THE COME BACK**

All of the things I said,
All of the things I did,
You came back for me,
And Your love was never hid.

You came back for me!!

You looked beyond my past,
You looked toward my future,
You changed my perspective,
And You gave me her.

You came back for me!!

I even stumbled,
I went off course,
You were still there,
You comforted my shame and hurt.

You came back for me!!

Nothing can stop Your love,
Your love for me,
It comes without criticism,
It comes so free.

You came back for me!!

I can now smile,
I know You are for me,
My dreams are in my eyes,
And I know You will always come back for me!!

FAITH

## GRACE

It covers my empty space,
It takes the pain away.
It takes me beyond what I imagined,
It allows me to see new horizons.

"That Grace"

It pulls me up when I am down,
It won't even let me drown.
It causes me to praise,
It makes worship a part of my days.

"That Grace"

It cleanses me from sin,
It keeps my light from going dim.
It puts food on the table,
It proves to me that God is able.

"That Grace"

It's what I need to live,
There aren't enough words to what it gives.
It's right on time and in place,
The only thing I can say is "That Grace."

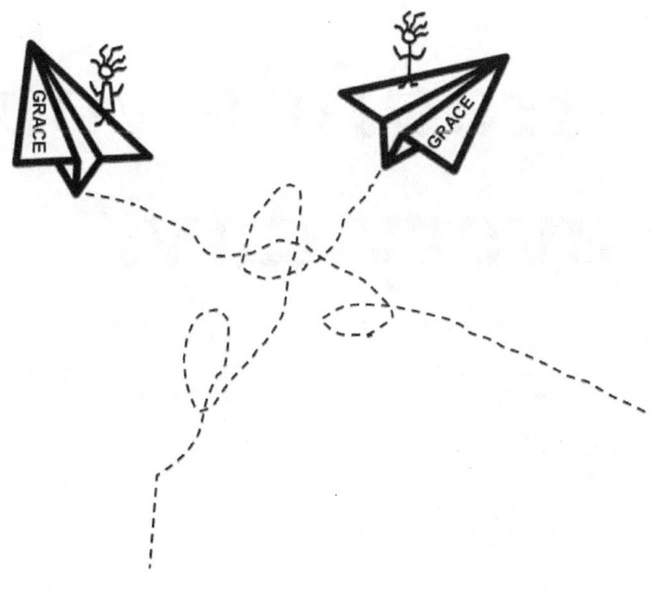

"GRACE
surrounds you
every day."

## BREAKER

God can break things in your life,
He can remove people and situations out of sight.
Break up bad relationships, habits and thoughts,
Release you from the past that you fought.

God is a stronghold breaker without a doubt,
He can even change what comes out of your mouth.
There is nothing too big for God, whether day or night,
God is the All Mighty that can break things in your life.

## CLEANER

Wiped clean with no trace,
No past history or words to waste.
What happened before doesn't matter,
Its what's before me that matters.

Now anew with the road ahead,
Speaking of what's possible and not what's dead.
No more pity on myself,
God took away the pain that I felt.

Hating me for what I've done came to an end,
Now it's time to see what begins.
I learn from life like learning from a teacher,
Thank You God for being my cleaner.

**"God chose you for a**

**REASON."**

## MY CHOICE

God covers everything I do,
He's a trusting friend through and through.
He gives me peace when negativity comes,
He calms my seas when things come undone.

God sits high and looks low,
He watches over me when I go.
No need to worry or to stress,
God always knows what's best.

God gives me glory day after day,
Even when I'm sleep, glory is in place.
No matter what I face, God won't le me lose,
It's all up to me and God's victory is what I choose.

## LIFEGUARD

With great hesitation, I stepped out of the boat,
I couldn't believe Jesus was calling me, but I had hope.
One foot in front of the other, this was becoming real,
I too was walking on water, oh so unreal.

My eyes were on Jesus as I walked His way,
Then I heard a wind as a storm was coming my way.
Terrified of this reality, I began to sink,
Water was over my head and I was going down deep.

All of a sudden, I felt a hand pull me up,
I was out of the water, laying in the boat and
that wasn't pure luck.
My Lifeguard look at me and said, "Why did you
have so little faith,"
Fear may have gotten the best of me, but I was the second
person to walk on water that amazing day.

**"You don't have to figure out life, just**

# LEARN

**from it."**

## MORE THAN ENOUGH

God, how can I face them, I don't have enough,
But if I have this and that, I will have enough.
What do You mean that's too much,
If I go any lower, I will be crushed.

Ok, if they aren't for me, I will let them go,
Now more than half rolled out and were on their way home.
It's going to be hard, but this will work I suppose,
God, what do you mean No!

You want me to let go even more,
The "no value added" ones left and I was on the floor.
God, how can I succeed with only this,
God said, "300 is enough because all you really need
is Me to handle all of this."

**+ GOD = MORE THAN ENOUGH**

## ALL KNOWING

You know what's best for me,
Your view is beyond what I can see.
You are wiser than all that I know,
Your direction is the best way I can go.

"God knows"

God can open doors that are further than my reach,
Your strength is greater than the examples that we speak.
There is no one more wonderful than You,
Forgive us for what we think we knew.

"God knows"

Our knowledge is dust compared to Yours,
Comprehending a piece of Your teaching leaves us floored.
Thank You for the wisdom that You provide,
I constantly seek Your help because God knows
where peace resides.

**"God doesn't always give an answer, but a**

# DIRECTION

**to follow."**

## A FRIEND

Jesus is a friend like no other,
He walks with me when my life is filled with clutter.
He brings peace in the room when I struggle,
He calms my stress when it's wrapped up in bundles.

Jesus is a friend by my side,
My past and sins from Him I do not hide.
He doesn't pass judgement on me,
He speaks words of wisdom and forgives me.

Jesus is a friend in the night,
When lust creeps in unseen by sight.
I just call His name and the thoughts flee,
Yes Jesus is a friend, a true friend to me.

## HOLY SPIRIT

There is this voice that continues to speak,
It comes to me in those moments when I'm weak.
It gives me direction when I am lost,
It comes to me no matter the cost.

This voice is hard to explain,
It's like it originates from my heart and goes to my brain.
It doesn't yell, but whispers like a love song,
Even though it's quiet, there is power in its resolve.

Jesus said He would leave someone here for us,
I wonder if this voice is just here for us.
We know that Jesus now reigns on high,
But He left His voice here still talking into our lives.

**"No one wants**
**to see you**
# WIN
**more than God."**

## #1 FAN

It's amazing we work so hard to please others,
When we have a #1 Fan that is above all others.
He's not worried about how popular you are,
To Him you're perfect, blessed and smart.

He celebrates all that you do,
He doesn't focus on the awards given to you.
He has His own rewards that He provides,
He gives what will impact the inside.
It won't just fill a spot on a bookshelf or wind up in a box,
He applies things to your life that can't be stopped.

Yes, you have a #1 Fan,
He has a smile on His face and applauding with his hands.
No matter what people say, He's on your side,
He's your #1 Fan that looks down from on high.

## VALUABLE

Our conversations are so simple yet deep,
When we talk, I don't even want to leave.
You have me thinking like I never have,
Your wisdom is so overwhelming, sometimes
it makes me laugh.

"You are Valuable"

Your words make me adjust my perception,
It's like I'm always in school and the teacher
has a great lesson.
You change my choices and decisions,
I want this every day, none of this do I want to go missing.

"You are Valuable"

I know some people have a lot of money but
they don't have this,
I will sacrifice great financial success for this.
What You give is fulfilling, joyous and sensational,
No other way to say it but You are Valuable!

**"Your worth is greater than your**

# **WALK."**

## RISING SON

Life is getting dark and it's hard to see,
The stress is building so high it's difficult to breathe.
This fight I am losing because I am the only one,
But I know light is coming because soon there will
be the rising of the Son.

Fear tries to claim victory and claim my territory,
I can't give in and let this be the end of my story.
Change has to come even though it hasn't begun,
But I know light is coming because soon there
will be the rising of the Son.

The horizon has so much to offer,
I feel hope knowing I won't always suffer.
I praise now in the lack of joy and fun,
But I know light is coming because soon there
will be the rising of the Son.

## CONTENT WATERS

Your blessings overtake me like a wave,
Currents of joy causes me to praise and shake.
The depths of Your love are too much,
My sea of emotions has never been so touched.

"Content Waters"

I want to sink in the grace that You give,
Oceans of favor do I embrace and feel.
No shallow love can be found here,
This is the deep stuff, beautiful and clear.

"Content Waters"

God is present because I feel the sands of life,
Its hard to contain the lakes leaving my sight.
God makes sure I lack nothing in these calming rivers,
Thank You God for all You do, my Content Waters.

**"Jesus loves you without LIMITS."**

## MY LOVER

This place is like no other,
Peace is at the core of My Lover.
A sense of safety and calm,
I know I'm wrapped in My Lover's arms.

"Oh, this Place"

Joy fills my spirit without doubt,
Thanks sound my lips and continue to come out.
My Lover knows I need this,
I let go of all my troubles and don't resist.

"Oh, this Place"

The touch is so real and unreal,
There is no mistaking the way I feel.
Further do I want to go with no time to waste,
My Lover, My Jesus is right here in this place.

## BIGGER THAN ME

Fear is trying to come my way,
It tries to steal my dreams and stop me when I pray.

"But there is someone Bigger than me"

Doubt tries to creep in like a thief,
Worry tries to bring me to my knees.

"But there is someone Bigger than me"

Criticism comes without remorse,
Constantly attacking to make my confidence hoarse.

"But there is someone Bigger than me"

No matter how strong the enemy comes, God is there,
He shoots his best shot, but God doesn't care.

"But there is someone Bigger than me"

The enemy turns back, runs and flees,

Because when he comes against me, he knows there is someone Bigger than me.

**"With God,**

# SIZE

**doesn't matter."**

## THE RISER

One step, two steps, the closer I arrive,
This day was meant for death, but this day I rise.
People look on cheering and booing,
But Father, they don't know what they are doing.

I'm going through this for all of them,
The thief, liar, adulterer, cheater, lust seeker and every sin.
This was My way to understand their pain,
It was also an opportunity to show how I played the life game.

I was an example, and I hope it worked,
Some will follow later, even though now they taunt.
If not this generation, the next generation will change,
I rise for the fallen when they confess My name.

## CITY DWELLER

What You are asking for is greater than I can think,
This cup is so large you need help to drink.
Don't get weary in your faith, it's just the enemy,
For this type of blessing, Jesus has to lead you out of the city.

There is a pain you never had before,
The slightest movement shakes you to your core.
You seek God for a healing because of His love and sympathy,
For this type of blessing, Jesus has to lead you out of the city.

It's your mother and you don't think she will make it,
The stress  is so heavy that your children can feel it.
You know God can do anything with a power that is infinity,
For this type of blessing, Jesus has to lead you out of the city.

**"No problems are too small or too**

# BIG

**for God."**

## VICTORY

I thank You for every victory You have sent my way,
You take me from Glory to Glory day after day.
Another accomplishment You place in my reach,
So many blessings, a count is hard to keep.

Victory, Victory, Victory!!

Further and further do I go,
High and higher does Your love flow.
You have provided more than I can think or ask,
I'm living beyond my wish list, how can I do the math.

Victory, Victory, Victory!!

What type of place will You put me in next,
I've already accepted my lot in life, but what will You do next.
I'm excited about my journey and the anointed story,
All I can say is God has given me Victory, Victory, Victory!!

## MY GOD, HIS NAMES OUTRO

I want to Thank You again for allowing this book to a part of your journey. I hope it made an impact or reminded you of the wonders of having God in your life. We are blessed to have Someone in our lives whose love does not fail. God's love is endless no matter how our past looks. May you reread the poems in this book, share them with others, or read them at events or open mics. I pray these words touch those God intended for them to reach.

If you want to know God or want a closer relationship with God, say the prayer below:

**"God, forgive me of my sins. I confess with my mouth and believe in my heart that You are my God, and Jesus died for my sins. Walk with me so I can become who You designed me to be. From this day forward, I am saved! Amen."**

Welcome to a new relationship with God! Talk with Him just like you talk to a friend about anything, anywhere, and watch the relationship grow. He is with you Always! God bless.

**"A new beginning starts when you**

# TALK

**to God."**

# ABOUT THE AUTHOR

Ryan "Jenks" Jenkins currently resides in the Hampton Roads area of Virginia. Jenks is a sought-after Life Speaker and author. He enjoys partnering with non-profits, churches, and schools. Jenks gets his Life Speaking messages across by using speeches, workshops, poetry, and books. In 2010, Jenks published his first book, *Life is a Motivational Speech.* This book inspires people to go after their goals and dreams in life and demonstrates how to learn from the experiences in life.

In the following years, Jenks published *Filthy Rags,* a testimony of everyday life challenges and how his faith helped him overcome them. These books were followed by *Single Again, The CHEAPS,* and many others. The information from Jenks' books is used for youth events and adult workshops that he facilitates. He has also held Author Workshops to help aspiring authors self-publish their books. Jenks has also been a celebrated member of Toastmasters International. He believes "There are no mistakes in life, just opportunities to become better."

Jenks is a proud husband, and father to three daughters. As Jenks was growing up, his increasing ambition and faith led him to the many accomplishments he has achieved in his life. His drive also led him to successfully graduate from Old Dominion University with a bachelor's degree in Electrical Engineering Technology. Jenks fulfilled one of his dreams by traveling around the U.S. for various engineering companies. Through seeing his past dreams come true, he now uses that as fuel to show others their dreams can come true also.

As a writer, Jenks has been writing poetry and speeches for over twenty years. He believes that "Everyone has a success story." Jenks was a long-time radio personality on the talk show "Church Talk in the Barbershop" with Bishop J.L. Johnson. You can also find him on other radio shows and discussion panels. Jenks' speaking style is true to the heart and well-received.

Growing as an entrepreneur, Jenks created a ministry/organization called "Poetic Souls Inc." (PSI). PSI had programs designed to build up people and communities. Its mission statement was "Inspiring the world through poetry..." PSI services include open mics, motivational speaking, MC

(Master of Ceremony), and workshops. PSI's first program was an inspirational poetry night called "The Poetic Souls Experience." This uplifting, expressive, and emotional open mic has been held in different venues throughout the East Coast. PSI has also supported various religious, community, and organizational events for AIDS, Multiple Sclerosis (MS), Hurricane Katrina, and the homeless. It has also worked with organizations such as the YMCA and Tidewater Arts Outreach youth programs.

If you would like Jenks to be a speaker at your next event, please send a request to JenRyan Company at JenRyanCompany@gmail.com or call (757) 318-1241. Let his words be a blessing to fill the time you have allotted. No program too big or too small! Jenks looks forward to serving you in the near future. May God bless you and remember to "Speak Life!"

# OTHER BOOKS BY RYAN "JENKS" JENKINS

**"Life is a Motivational Speech" © 2010**

**"Filthy Rags: Everybody is Fighting Something" © 2011**

**"Single Again: Friendships, Relationships & Marriage" © 2012**

**"The CHEAPS: Why Spend It If You Don't Have To" © 2012**

"Move Maker's Handbook: Lessons Learned from an Entrepreneur and Dreamer." © 2014

"Living a Lime Green Life: Quotes, Thoughts and Theories" © 2014

"The Marriage Retreat: Setting the Mood for Passion" © 2015

"Watch Out For Me: Just Letting the Ladies Know" © 2015

"Let's Talk Men: It's Time to Come Clean" © 2015

"LEAD: Listen, Empower, And Deliver" © 2020

"You Are WEIRD: Embracing the Real YOU" © 2020

"Different: Memoirs of a Difference Maker" © 2020

**"Express It: Faith, Poetry, Art, etc." © 2021**

**"Free to Profit: Giving Into Your Future" © 2021**

**"Forty Words: Writer's Challenge and Expressions" © 2021**

**"Kids Speak Life: 12 Affirmations" © 2022**

**"What's Next: The Journey into Adulting and Self-Reliance" © 2022**

Books are available to purchase online at
www.amazon.com/author/ryanjenksjenkins

www.ingramcontent.com/pod-product-compliance
Lightning Source LLC
LaVergne TN
LVHW091123150826
845673LV00002B/950

* 9 7 9 8 8 4 6 3 1 2 3 4 0 *